TABLE OF CONTENTS

CHAPTER I

VOLLEYBALL DREAMS

When the school bell rang, Layla Sanchez hustled from her last class to the girls' locker room. She quickly changed into shorts and a tank top. She pulled her socks up over her calves and slid on her kneepads. Once her long, straight brown hair was in a ponytail, she entered the gym for volleyball practice.

During the season, Layla was always first to the gym, aside from Coach Eagan. Before her teammates arrived, Layla thought about the season and her long-term goals. As she walked across the gleaming floor, she remembered the cheering crowds from past games. She grabbed a volleyball from the ball rack and imagined running onto the court for the next Lincoln Middle School Lions game. Next year, she hoped to play at the high school. After that, she'd be on a college team. Eventually, she imagined, she'd be on the U.S. National Team.

Could it really happen? Could my dreams really come true? she wondered. Layla's stomach flipped with nervous excitement.

Layla twirled the volleyball in her hands as she jogged toward a nearby wall. She tossed the ball into the air and smacked it down at an angle so that it hit the ground, then the wall, and then bounced back to her. To make her lifelong dreams come true, Layla would need to work hard on her skills, especially this year. This was Layla's last season before trying out for the high school team. Playing as a freshman was the next step in her big plan.

Layla heard her teammates chatting and laughing.

She turned toward the locker room doors as they entered the gym.

"There she is—Layla 'Ace' Sanchez!" said Kristy Thompson, Layla's best friend.

Layla smiled. Then, to prove she deserved the nickname, she shuffled back to get more distance from the wall. She bounced the ball four times, then tossed it high and a few feet in front of her. Layla jumped up and forward. She hit the ball with her palm, driving it into the base of the wall. When the ball bounced back to her, her teammates cheered and clapped.

"What's with all the noise?" asked Coach Eagan, who had come out of her office. She put her clipboard and cell phone on a small table near the door. She walked toward the group of excited girls and said, "I thought this was practice, not a rock concert."

"Did you see Layla's killer jump serve, Coach?" asked Kristy. "It gets better every week! That's why we're undefeated!" Kristy gave Layla a high-five.

"I love the enthusiasm," said Coach Eagan, "but

we have lots of tough games ahead of us. We can't count only on Layla's killer jump serve."

Layla's cheeks warmed. *Did she think I was showing off?* Layla wondered. *I hope not.* Layla liked her teammates' praise, but she didn't want to act like a diva, especially not in front of the new sixth-grade players. Layla's dad had talked to her a lot about being a true team player.

"We all have to be at our best, so let's get to work," said Coach.

The girls groaned but quickly spread out to start warm-up drills. Coach Eagan led the players through quad stretches, toy soldier kicks, and shuffles. In the middle of a shuffle, Coach's cell phone rang.

"Sorry girls, but I have to answer that," Coach Eagan said. "I'm expecting a call from the high school coach." She jogged toward her phone.

Layla and Kristy exchanged a look. Layla felt the butterflies in her stomach again. Before she answered the call, Coach Eagan said, "Layla, please take over."

"Yes, Coach," Layla said and ran to the front of the group. "Okay, everyone, let's do squats."

Layla did the squats along with the others. First, she swung her arms in big backward circles. Then, she spread her feet wider than shoulder-width apart. She lowered herself like she was sitting in a chair. She held her arms straight out in front of her for balance. After several squats, Layla looked over at Coach Eagan. She was still on the phone.

"Okay, pick a partner and start passing drills," Layla called out.

Layla and Kristy paired up. Layla stood up straight with her back to the net. Kristy stood about eight feet away, facing Layla. Kristy crouched down in the ready position. Kristy's feet were shoulder-width apart, and her knees were slightly bent. Her arms were bent at the elbows. Her hands were flat and straight, ready to join together when the ball reached her. With two hands, Layla tossed the ball to Kristy in a gentle underhanded arc. Kristy brought her arms together and straightened them. Her wrists and hands were together, her thumbs side by side, and her elbows were locked. She used the flat platform of her forearms to bump the ball back to Layla.

After a few passes, Layla glanced at Coach Eagan. "I'm dying to know what they're talking about," she said to Kristy.

"Me too," said Kristy as she bumped the ball back to Layla.

Layla twirled the ball in her hands and yelled, "Switch!" Everyone changed positions with their partners and started the drill again. Now Kristy tossed the ball to Layla, who bumped it back to Kristy.

After a few more minutes, Coach Eagan ended the call and walked toward the girls. She thanked Layla for taking over warm-ups and asked the girls to circle up in front of her.

"I'm sorry about that, but like I said, I was expecting that call from Coach Keating. She plans to attend some of our games and may visit during practices," Coach said. "She wants to check out possible players for next year's freshman team."

Layla and Kristy exchanged excited looks.

"She also wanted me to remind the eighth graders about the C rule," said Coach.

Layla's stomach dropped.

"We know, Coach," said Maggie Jones, an eighth grader.

"Well, I'm still going to remind you," said Coach. "Actually, it's the perfect time for a refresher because we're about halfway through the season and the first quarter of school," said Coach. "Simply put, you must maintain at least a C in all of your classes at all times to participate in any extra activities. That means at least a seventy percent. If your average in a class slips below that, you won't be allowed to practice or play until you raise your grade."

Kristy shrugged like this was no big deal, but Layla sucked in a deep breath and let it out slowly.

"The high school also has the C rule, so we want

you to get used to it now," said Coach Eagan. "You *must* learn how to balance sports and academics."

Coach Eagan waited a few moments. "Any questions?" When no one spoke up, she said, "Then let's get back to work."

* * *

At the end of practice, Layla and Kristy walked across the gym toward the locker room.

"Are you excited about Coach Keating coming?" asked Kristy.

"Of course," said Layla. "I'm a little nervous too."

"Nervous? You're Ace Sanchez! You have nothing to worry about," Kristy said. Then she jumped and yelled "Boom!" as she pretended to hit a volleyball the way Layla did earlier.

Layla laughed. "I'm worried about the C rule."

"Oh!" Kristy scrunched up her nose and asked, "Math?"

Layla nodded. "I already have a low C, and it's only going to get harder." Layla's voice was a whisper when she added, "My dad used to help me with math."

Kristy reached for Layla's hand and squeezed it gently. Layla squeezed back before she let go.

"Well, I can tutor you in algebra, and you can help me with my serve!" Kristy said. "We would be unstoppable on and off the court!"

Layla laughed as they walked into the locker room. "I'll think about it," she said, but all Layla really wanted to think about was making it onto the freshman team. Algebra would have to wait until she could show off her volleyball skills for the high school coach.

CHAPTER 2

COMMUNICATION AND TRUST

That night, Layla sat at the desk in her room doing homework. She finished a worksheet of grammar practice for English and answered questions about the U.S. Constitution for history. She saved algebra for last. When she finally opened her textbook and read the first problem, she instantly felt frustrated. It was about a boy named Jack who wanted to build a tree house. He had a certain amount of lumber and needed to cut it into different sizes. Layla was supposed to come up with the equation and solve it.

Dad would've used toothpicks or Legos or something, Layla thought. She looked around the room but didn't see anything she could use as a prop. *Even if I did find something, what would I do with it?* she thought. *Dad was the master at this stuff, not me.*

Layla considered asking her mom for help, then laughed. Her dad's voice echoed in her head: "I'm like a straight line. Mom's like a pinball machine."

Yup, step-by-step is not Mom's thing, Layla thought. *That's why Dad was my homework helper.* Layla slammed the textbook shut and turned on her laptop. She had one tab open to a math practice site and another open to highlights of the U.S. Women's National Volleyball Team. They had played Brazil in the last Women's World Cup in Japan.

Layla muted the sound in case her mom came upstairs. Layla loved how the U.S. National Team moved on the court. They were a well-oiled machine. Each player had her individual job, but they all worked together toward a common goal. Layla's team did that too, but sometimes they still gave up easy points.

Communication and trust are important, in the game and in life. That's what her dad used to say. He had been gone for two years now, and Layla missed him every day.

Layla's eyes filled with tears. She quickly wiped them away. *Focus on the game,* she told herself. That usually helped to push away the sadness.

A U.S. player's serve was returned by the Brazilian team in three hits—dig, set, spike. The U.S. libero dropped to her knees and made contact, but the ball went backward and out of bounds. The U.S. setter ran to the ball and bumped it hard back into play. The right-side hitter got under the ball, jumped high, and spiked it. The Brazilian libero dove for the ball but couldn't keep it in play. Point for Team U.S.A.!

Layla wanted to turn on the sound to listen to the commentary, but she heard her mom's footsteps on the stairs. She knew her mom would come into her room before going to bed. It was part of her nightly routine. When her mom was almost at the door, Layla clicked on the other tab on her laptop to display the math practice site.

"It's getting late," her mom said. "Are you almost done with your homework?"

"Almost," Layla said.

"Well, finish up and get a good night's sleep."

"I will," said Layla.

Mom crossed the room and kissed Layla on top of her head. "Good night. Love you."

"Love you too," said Layla.

When she heard her mom's bedroom door close, Layla shoved her books into her backpack and shut down her laptop. She climbed into bed with her cell phone and turned away from the door. If her mom peaked in again, Layla would look like she was sleeping.

Layla went online and kept watching volleyball highlights on her phone until her eyelids became so heavy she had to close them. As she fell asleep, she dreamed about one day being on that court in front of thousands of cheering fans. Since it was a dream, both of her parents were there.

CHAPTER 3

UNDER CONTROL

The next morning, Layla bounded down the stairs and into the kitchen.

"Good morning, sweetie," Mom said as she poured herself a cup of coffee.

"Good morning," said Layla. She plopped her backpack onto the floor and checked inside to make sure she had everything she needed.

"Did you finish all of your homework last night?" Mom asked.

"Yup," Layla said.

I mean, no! she screamed in her head. She hadn't planned to lie, but it was too late. She remembered her dad's words about communication and trust. *I'll make this right,* she said to herself. *I'll finish my homework before math class. Then the lie won't count. I just need to learn how to balance everything, like Coach said.*

"And do you have what you need for volleyball practice?" Mom put her coffee mug on the counter and handed Layla a lunch bag.

Layla nodded. "Everything's in my gym locker," she said.

"Good! I'm so proud of how you're handling all of your responsibilities this year," her mom said, smiling.

Layla gave her a weak smile.

"Eighth grade can be tough," Mom said, "and you seem to have everything under control."

If I had everything under control, my homework would be done, my math average would be at least a B, and I wouldn't have lied! Layla thought. She swallowed hard, but the lump in her throat didn't budge.

Layla put her lunch bag into her backpack and zipped it up. She put her arms through the straps and lifted it onto her back. She gave her mom a quick kiss on the cheek, grabbed a granola bar from the pantry, and said, "Bye, Mom. Have a good day at work."

"Bye. Have a great day at school."

On the bus, Layla opened her backpack and pulled out her algebra textbook, a notebook, and a pencil. Layla sat with her back to the bus window and tried to balance the textbook and notebook on her lap. She needed to finish her homework from the night before. Layla complained each time the bus hissed to a hard stop or hit a bump in the road.

"What the heck?!" Layla shouted.

Kristy sat in the seat across the aisle from Layla. She shook her head and said, "You're not going to be able to do your homework on the bus."

"Oh yeah? Watch me," said Layla.

As the bus stopped and started along its route, Layla's pencil jammed into the notebook and her book kept falling onto the floor.

"We need a better driver," said Layla.

"The problem isn't the driver," Kristy said. "The work is hard. I spent a half hour on that assignment last night."

"I have more than a half hour between now and when school starts."

"Yeah, but—" Before Kristy could finish her sentence, the bus jolted again as it hit a pothole.

Layla's book bounced off the seat and onto the floor.

"I rest my case," said Kristy.

Layla shoved her work into her backpack. She was annoyed with the bus driver for not giving her a smoother ride to school. She was annoyed with Kristy for acting like a know-it-all. She was annoyed with herself for not doing her homework the night before.

Most of all, she was annoyed with algebra. She didn't care about finding X or solving for Y. She would never use this in her life . . . ever!

CHAPTER 4

HOMEWORK CHECK

Layla raced through the hallways to get to her locker. She quickly unloaded everything from her backpack and took out what she needed for her first few classes. She zoomed into homeroom. She hoped to finish her homework during the fifteen minutes used for attendance and announcements.

Another student, Henry, had the same idea. He had the grammar worksheet on his desk. Just as he was about to start working, Mr. Miller said, "Please put that away, Henry. A student council representative is coming to give us an update on school events. I expect all of you to give him your full attention."

Henry groaned as he put away his homework.

Great, thought Layla. *First the bus driver was against me. Now Mr. Miller and the student council are ruining my plan.* Layla wouldn't have time to finish her homework, and algebra was her first-period class.

Layla walked into her math class feeling defeated. She took a "warm-up" sheet from the paper tray on Mrs. Fisher's desk and slid into her assigned seat. Each day, students worked on the warm-up problem while Mrs. Fisher stopped at their desks to check their homework.

Layla hunched over and shook her head so that her hair fell around her face. Even though she was trying to hide, she knew she couldn't avoid getting in trouble with both Mrs. Fisher and her mom. Lincoln Middle School had a computerized grading system that updated as soon as teachers put in new grades. Her mom would know that Layla received a zero for the homework she'd said was done. She'd be in trouble for not doing the work and for lying. Layla clutched her stomach. *Mom has been through enough the last few years. I don't want to hurt her even more or give her something new to worry about.*

Layla opened her notebook to the page that should've displayed her homework. She pushed the notebook to the upper right corner of her desk and stared at the warm-up problem. When Mrs. Fisher was next to Layla's desk, Layla kept her eyes down and focused on her paper.

Mrs. Fisher tapped her pencil's eraser on top of Layla's notebook. "What's this, Ms. Sanchez?"

Layla sat up straight and looked at Mrs. Fisher. The page was blank except for yesterday's date and smudge marks made from writing and erasing numbers. "I had trouble with the homework," she said.

"I see that. What exactly was the problem?"

"All of it," said Layla.

"I doubt that," said Mrs. Fisher. "You should've been able to do *some* of it."

Layla didn't say anything.

"Ms. Sanchez, you should at least make an attempt," said Mrs. Fisher. "Do what you can, even if it's only part of each problem. Then ask questions about what you don't understand. This," Mrs. Fisher tapped her eraser on the empty page again, "looks like you didn't even try."

Layla sighed. "You're right," she admitted. "I'm sorry. Can I come in at lunch to make up the work?"

"Yes, but you'll receive only half credit since it wasn't finished at the start of class."

"Okay," said Layla. *Half credit is better than a zero*, she thought.

"I'll see you at lunch, Ms. Sanchez." Mrs. Fisher continued to circle the room. In a loud voice, she said, "Class, let me remind you why homework is important."

Layla rolled her eyes. She already felt guilty about

lying to her mom and not doing the work. Now she had to give up lunch with her friends to work with Mrs. Fisher on algebra. She wasn't in the mood for a lecture too.

"Your homework is practice for future quizzes and tests," Mrs. Fisher said. "If you don't do your homework, you may struggle later."

Mrs. Fisher completed her homework check and stood at the front of the classroom. She looked directly at Layla and said, "Math is kind of like playing a sport."

Layla's face must have twitched or made an *Are you kidding me?* kind of look because Mrs. Fisher asked, "You don't believe me, Ms. Sanchez?"

Layla's cheeks warmed with embarrassment. She shrugged and said, "I don't know."

"Well, if one of your teammates doesn't attend any practices, will she do well in the games?" asked Mrs. Fisher.

"Probably not," said Layla.

"And if she can't handle the ball in basic ways, will she be able to do more advanced moves?"

"Definitely not," said Layla.

"Math is similar. If you don't master the basics, you can't master more advanced skills," said Mrs. Fisher. "And if you don't practice, you won't perform well when it really counts."

Mrs. Fisher walked to a large calendar hanging on the wall. "Speaking of things that really count, the unit test is next Friday. Please take out your agendas."

Layla opened her binder and took out her school-issued agenda. She flipped the pages until she got to the right place.

Layla had already written *volleyball practice* in the "after school" area for every Monday, Tuesday, and Thursday during the volleyball season. She also wrote in the place and time for each game.

"The unit test will be a major grade for the first quarter," said Mrs. Fisher. "I'm handing out a review packet today. I'm also offering extra help sessions after school. The first is tomorrow."

Layla sighed. She knew Mrs. Fisher's comment about keeping up with the homework was aimed at her. She also knew that she had to do better in math to keep playing volleyball. *I can't fall below a C average,* she told herself. *I don't want to disappoint everyone—my teammates, Coach, Mom, or myself. And, Dad, even though you're not here, I don't want to disappoint you either.* She wrote *algebra review session* in her agenda for Wednesday after school.

"The next after-school session is Friday," said Mrs. Fisher. "And the third is next Wednesday, two days before the test."

Layla wrote those down too. She wasn't thrilled about spending three days after school reviewing algebra with Mrs. Fisher, but she needed the extra help before the test. *At least the sessions won't conflict with volleyball,* Layla thought as she put her agenda away.

CHAPTER 5

MATH VS. VOLLEYBALL

"Hey, where were you at lunch?" Kristy asked Layla at the start of volleyball practice that afternoon.

"I had to make up my algebra homework with Mrs. Fisher," said Layla.

"I don't want to say 'I told you so,' but . . ."

"Then don't," said Layla with a smile.

"Get ready for warm-ups!" Coach called out. Layla and Kristy moved to an open space on the gym floor.

As they waited for Coach Eagan to call out the first stretch, Kristy said, "The tutoring offer still stands.

I mean, I don't want to brag, but guess who's got an A in algebra? This girl!" Kristy jabbed both of her thumbs into her chest.

"Of course you do," Layla said. "Thanks, but I don't want to talk about algebra anymore."

Coach Eagan led the girls through a series of dynamic stretches and then split them up into two teams, six on each side.

"Today we're going to work on our serves," said Coach Eagan.

"Awww yeah!" called out Layla.

Everyone laughed.

"The serve is the one thing you can control completely during the game," said Coach Eagan. "It's the only time you're not reacting to another player's move. Not only do you want to get the ball over the net, but you want to aim it too." Coach Eagan moved closer to Layla and said, "I'll use Layla as my model."

Layla struck a quick pose like a runway model before getting into the correct serving position.

"She's standing at a forty-five-degree angle," Coach Eagan said. "Her right shoulder is back, and her weight is on her right foot in back. The ball is in her left hand in front of her, not too low. She's going to lift the ball no more than two feet above her."

Layla lifted the ball into the air and let it drop. She'd done countless lift drills to perfect her serve. Having a good lift was an important first step.

"She's going to step into the lift, turn at the hip, and drag her right toe forward," Coach continued. "Finally, she's going to hit the ball right in the center with a strong, flat palm. Don't follow through with your arm, and don't jump. This is a standing float serve."

"You want me to hit it now?" Layla asked.

"Go for it," said Coach. "And aim it at Thompson."

Kristy got into ready position on the other side of the net. "Bring it, Sanchez," she said.

Layla bounced the ball before she followed each of the steps Coach described. She lifted the ball, shifted her weight, and hit it hard. The ball moved through the air like a knuckleball and headed straight for Kristy in the middle of the back row.

Kristy got low and under the ball. With strong, straight arms, she bumped the ball high into the air. Another player caught it.

Everyone clapped.

Coach said, "Nice job, ladies. Now Kristy, switch places with Grace next to you. Watch how Layla pivots her body just enough to aim it at Kristy in her new position. She's also going to do a jump serve now."

"Why me, Coach?" Kristy whined. Everyone laughed.

"You can take it, Thompson!" Layla said. "Get ready."

"The jump serve has topspin, so it can be hard to return," said Coach.

Layla took three steps back and bounced the ball on the floor.

"Oh, boy," Kristy said as she got into her ready position.

"Layla is going to face where she wants the ball to go, so she'll turn toward Kristy slightly. She'll toss the ball, take three steps, and this time, she'll jump to hit and swing her arm through after hitting the ball," said Coach. "Ready, girls?"

"Ready," Layla and Kristy said at the same time.

Layla tossed the ball, took three steps, jumped high, and smacked it over the net. The ball came at Kristy fast and hard. She got low again, but this serve was more powerful. Kristy made contact with the ball, but it flew out of bounds. Kristy smacked the gym floor in frustration. When she stood up, she said, "I'm glad we're on the same team, Ace."

"Okay, ladies. Let's play," said Coach Eagan. "I want to see good skills in all positions, but especially when it's your turn to serve. Pay attention to your form. Everyone should try both a float and jump serve. Also, work on shifting your body to aim your serve at players on the other side of the net. This comes in handy in games when you notice a weak spot. Do more than get it over the net. Be strategic."

Layla's side rotated clockwise. A girl named Talia got ready to serve. She bounced the ball a few times and then executed a perfect float serve.

Grace Velez, a sixth grader, dropped to one knee for a dig that sailed back over the net. Talia bumped the ball high with a slight arc toward Maggie, the middle blocker in the front row. Maggie turned around and bumped the ball to the right. A girl named Ella jumped straight up and, instead of spiking the ball, gently tapped it over the net to an open area.

Layla's side cheered the point, while the other side moaned and chatted about being aware of unguarded spaces.

When Talia got the ball back, she bounced it a few times before attempting a jump serve. Her angle was off when she hit it, so the ball sailed right into the net.

The other side rotated. Grace smacked the ball as she bounced it. She lifted the ball and hit it over the net. Layla was ready for the pass. She bumped the ball and aimed it at Maggie. Instead of setting up another player, Maggie turned around and bumped it backward over the net.

Kristy called for it and bumped it high to the player in front of her. The girl set the ball with her fingertips to the right-side hitter. The hitter spiked the ball over the net, but it was returned quickly with a bump. The ball headed back toward Layla. Her solid bump sent the ball back over the net. Grace took a step to the left, but she should have stepped right. When the ball hit her platform, it sailed out of bounds.

Layla's side clapped for getting back the serve. When Layla noticed the disappointed look on Grace's face, she yelled, "Nice hustle, Grace!"

At the end of practice, the girls circled around Coach Eagan. She said, "As you know, we don't have a game this Saturday. Next Saturday we play Ridgefield

Middle School and then Washington Middle School the following week."

The girls exchanged looks at the mention of Washington Middle School. Lincoln and Washington had been crosstown rivals for generations.

"To get ready for the Washington game, I'm going to open the gym on what are usually our days off. So, in addition to our regular practices on Mondays, Tuesdays, and Thursdays," Coach said, "I'll also be here Wednesdays and Fridays."

"So, you're basically going to live here, Coach?" asked Maggie.

"Yeah, basically," Coach said with a laugh. "You're not required to come to the extra sessions, but if you want to practice particular skills, I'll be here to help. Also, I let Coach Keating know about the extra practice sessions. She may stop by."

As the girls walked toward the locker room, Kristy said, "Those are the same days as Mrs. Fisher's review sessions."

"I know," said Layla.

"So, I think I'll go to Mrs. Fisher's review sessions for half of the time and then come here," said Kristy. "What about you?"

"I don't know yet," Layla said. As she changed and packed up, Layla's mind raced. *Why did the math review sessions have to be at the same time as the extra practices? Kristy's half-and-half idea makes sense, but what if I'm at the math review session when Coach Keating is at a practice? I need to get my grade up, but I don't want to miss a chance to meet the high school coach.*

As Layla walked to the bus, a planned formed. *I'll use online sites for extra help and review my notes every chance I get. I'm going to the extra practice sessions. I want to be ready for the big game against Washington, and I don't want to miss the chance to impress Coach Keating.*

CHAPTER 6

KITCHEN TABLE TALK

After the bus dropped her off, Layla pushed open the front door of her house and ran up the stairs two at a time. She yelled, "Hey, Mom!" when she was halfway up the steps. She hoped to delay the conversation she knew was coming. No such luck.

"Hold on!" Mom yelled back.

Layla was already on the top step. She slowly turned around and looked down at her mom. She stood at the bottom of the stairs. Her hands were balled into fists and firmly planted on her hips.

"What's up, Mom?" Layla asked. She forced her lips into a smile.

Mom made a motion with her hand. "Come on, Layla," she said. "Kitchen table time." Her mom didn't wait for Layla to respond. She walked toward the kitchen and expected Layla to follow.

A kitchen table talk was always more serious than a comfy couch chat. When they were both seated, Layla's mom said, "I checked your grades today."

Layla didn't respond.

"At the beginning of the year, you had a B average in algebra, which was great. But your average has dropped with each quiz."

"I had a B when we were reviewing everything from last year. That was easy," said Layla. "It's not easy anymore, and Dad's not here to help me."

Her mom's expression softened. "I know," she said. They were both quiet for a minute, then her mom asked, "So, what happened today? Why did you get half credit on yesterday's homework?"

"I did it, but I didn't hand it in on time."

"Why not?"

Layla froze for a second. *I should tell her the truth. But if I admit I lied about the homework, I'll be grounded. I can't risk missing volleyball. Not now.*

Layla was about to make something up, but the words *Communication and trust* ran through her mind. She couldn't lie again. She told her mom everything—that she didn't finish her homework, lied about it, and completed it during lunch.

"I'm sorry, Mom," said Layla. She braced herself for her punishment.

Mom stared at Layla for a long time before she stood and walked to the snack cabinet. When she came back with chocolate chip cookies, Layla was confused.

"Want some milk?" her mom asked.

"Yes, please," Layla said. She felt the knots in her stomach loosen.

Layla's mom got two glasses of milk. Then she

joined her daughter in dunking cookies until just before they fell apart.

"What's going on?" asked Layla.

"It's a kitchen table talk," said her mom. "We're talking . . . and having a snack."

"I'm not grounded?"

"I think the stress and guilt you felt all day, plus the half credit and lecture you got from Mrs. Fisher were enough."

Layla nodded and sighed. She could feel the tension drain from her body.

"Layla, I don't expect you to be a straight A student, but I do expect you to do your best work," her mom said. "If you tell me you're trying your hardest and you get a B or C, that's fine."

This had always been her mom's philosophy.

"Everyone has tough subjects. Science was my struggle. Can you believe that?" Mom moved her hand up and down the front of her nursing scrubs. "I studied twice as hard for science as I did for my other classes, and I still never got an A. I worked hard for whatever grades I got. I expect you to work hard too."

"I know," said Layla.

"How can I help you?" her mom asked.

"I don't want you to worry about me. I have a plan."

"Okay, then, I'll let you figure this out," her mom said. "But if you need me, I'm here for you."

"I know."

Mom smiled and said, "Watch, I bet after all this, you'll end up liking math."

Layla nearly choked on her cookie. "I don't think so," she said.

"Look what happened to me," Mom said. She dunked another cookie and looked a little sad. "When your dad got sick, I researched his illness and medications. After a while, I sounded and acted so much like his nurses that I decided to become one. That was the worst time in my life, but something good came from it."

"Uh, Mom?"

"Yeah?"

"Your cookie," Layla said.

Her mom pulled her hand up and held what was left of the cookie she had been dunking. They both laughed.

"No worries," said Mom. "I'll add ice, blend it, and make a chocolate-chip milkshake! Want one?"

"Yes!" said Layla.

"After you eat dinner and do *all* of your homework." She gave Layla a pointed look.

Layla nodded. "I'll try harder, Mom."

"Good. You're dangerously close to being in the D range. Every point will count if you want to keep playing volleyball."

Layla nodded. She knew her mom was right.

After dinner, Layla started her algebra review packet. *I can do this*, she thought. When she got stuck, she searched online math sites for help. She watched videos and took notes, but the information didn't always match up with the review packet. *Can I do this?* she wondered.

An hour later, she had a few answers, lots of questions, and the start of a headache. *That's enough,* she decided. She closed the math sites and opened a new tab. She spent the rest of the night watching online videos of the high school team's past games to better understand Coach Keating and her players.

CHAPTER 7

COACH MEETING

At the end of the next school day, Layla headed to the locker room to change for the drop-in volleyball session. She made sure to avoid walking past Mrs. Fisher's classroom.

When Layla entered the gym, she saw Grace practicing bump passes with Coach Eagan. Layla stopped in her tracks. She had always been the first player at practice.

"Hi, Layla," Grace said after bumping a ball back to Coach Eagan.

"Hey, Grace," said Layla.

Coach Eagan turned around and said, "She beat you to the gym, Sanchez."

"I see that," Layla said with a smile.

"It's a good sign for the program," said Coach Eagan. "We need dedicated sixth graders—especially since we're losing so many talented eighth graders after this year."

Layla didn't know what to say. She was excited about moving on to the high school team, but she'd also miss her coach and teammates.

Other players entered the gym to practice. "Hey, girls," Coach Eagan called. She tossed the ball to Layla and said, "Here. You work with Grace, and I'll work with them."

"Sure, Coach," Layla said.

Grace beamed. She was obviously excited to work one-on-one with Ace Sanchez.

Layla led Grace through knee passes. Grace had one knee on the floor and the other to her side. Just like when she was standing, Grace held her ready position. Layla tossed the ball underhanded. Grace put her arms and thumbs together and bumped it back to Layla. After several of those, Layla moved so that she was on one side of the net and Grace was on the other.

"I'm going to aim it at different spots on your side of the net. I'll call out left or right to give you a heads-up," said Layla.

"Got it," Grace said. She backed up and got in her ready position. Layla also backed up. She called out, "Right!" before lifting the ball and hitting it over the net toward Grace's right side. Grace shuffled to her right and bumped it straight up. She caught it and sent it back to Layla.

"Stay on the right side until I serve. It's going left, okay?" said Layla.

Grace nodded.

Layla didn't serve with her full strength, but she sent it far to the left, almost to the out-of-bounds line. Grace started to shuffle but realized she'd have to run to reach the ball before it hit the ground. With a foot of space left between the ball and the floor, Grace dove with her arm extended. Her closed fist made contact with the ball.

"Whoo-hoo!" Layla cheered.

Grace smiled as she picked herself up off the floor.

Just then, Coach Eagan and a woman Layla recognized as Coach Keating walked toward the girls.

"Time out, ladies," said Coach Eagan. "Coach Keating, this is Grace Velez. She's a scrappy sixth grader, as you just saw. She already has solid skills. You'll definitely want to come back and see her as an eighth grader."

Grace smiled and waved hello.

Layla's palms started to sweat as Coach talked about Grace. *This is it*, she thought. *Breathe and don't say anything stupid. Time to make a good impression.*

"And this is Layla Sanchez," Coach said. Layla wiped her palms on the sides of her shorts before shaking Coach Keating's hand.

"It's very nice to meet you, Layla. I've heard a lot about you. I hope you're interested in playing in high school."

"Yes, Coach," Layla said. "Definitely. I've even been watching videos of old high school games to understand the team and your coaching style."

"I'm impressed," said Coach Keating. "You must be dedicated to the sport if you're viewing past games and attending extra practice sessions."

Layla nodded. "I love volleyball. I hope to play professionally one day."

"Great. Well, one step at a time," said Coach Keating. "Your next step could very well be the freshman team if you stay on top of your skills and grades."

Layla's stomach muscles clenched in response to Coach Keating's comment. *Another reminder to balance school and sports.*

"It's nice to see you working with a younger player," said Coach Keating. Grace and Layla looked at each other and smiled. "That's the kind of teamwork and leadership I expect from my players."

Layla nodded and smiled.

"Well, nice to meet you both," said Coach Keating. She walked with Coach Eagan to the sidelines. They talked for a bit and then Coach Eagan brought out a chair from her office so Coach Keating could sit and watch the other girls practice.

Layla thought about Coach Keating's comments about keeping up her skills and grades. She also thought about Kristy splitting her time between Mrs. Fisher's review sessions and Coach Eagan's extra practices. *Now that I've met Coach Keating, I'll go to the other algebra review sessions*, Layla told herself.

But at the end of practice, Grace ran up to Layla's side. "Are you coming to the other drop-in sessions?" she asked. "I'd love help with my serve."

Layla looked at Grace's hopeful expression. Coach Eagan had said young, dedicated players like Grace were the future MVPs of the Lincoln Lions. Also,

Coach Keating expected older players to help younger ones. Her dad had always told her to be a true team player.

I'll keep using the online sites to review for algebra, she decided.

"I'll be here," said Layla.

"Really?" Grace asked as she bounced on her toes.

"Yes, I promise."

CHAPTER 8

RETAKE

The next Friday, Layla sat in her algebra class, staring at the unit test. She read the questions over and over. Some of it looked familiar because she always paid attention in class. She'd also done all the homework, as best she could, since the day she made up her work with Mrs. Fisher during lunch. She reviewed her notes and watched online tutorials.

But it wasn't enough.

Those online help sites weren't that helpful after all. I should've asked more questions in class. I should've let

Kristy tutor me. I should've attended the review sessions or asked Mom or Mrs. Fisher for help. Why did I think I could do this on my own?

Layla sighed heavily and did what she could, but she knew she was going to fail. Her math average would fall to a D. As she handed in her test, she thought, *I won't be able to practice today or play in tomorrow's game against Ridgefield. I'm going to let everyone down. I'm not a team leader. I'm a failure.*

A few periods later, Layla visited Mrs. Fisher during her study hall. Mrs. Fisher was hunched over a pile of tests, marking up answers in purple pen.

"I'm fast, but I'm not a machine," said Mrs. Fisher. "You won't have your grade until the end of the day."

"I know I failed," said Layla.

"And how do you know that?" asked Mrs. Fisher.

"I just know," said Layla.

Mrs. Fisher stopped correcting and removed her glasses. She motioned for Layla to sit at the desk in front of her.

Once Layla was seated, Mrs. Fisher asked, "So, what's going to happen now, Ms. Sanchez?"

"I won't be able to play in the game against Ridgefield tomorrow," Layla said. "It'll be my first time sitting out."

"I see," said Mrs. Fisher, "but I was referring to your math grade. What do you plan to do about that?"

"Could I retake the test on Monday?" asked Layla.

"You *could,* but I don't think a weekend of reviewing on your own is going to help," said Mrs. Fisher.

Layla sighed. "So what can I do?"

"You really have only one option. You need to learn the material from the master," Mrs. Fisher said and pointed at herself.

Layla laughed.

"The only way to do that," Mrs. Fisher continued, "is to work with me after school, starting today, until you're truly ready to retake the test."

"Okay," said Layla.

"After the retake, I'll average the two grades. Fair?"

Layla nodded again.

A good grade on the retake would get me back on the court in time for the game against the Washington Hawks. But what if Coach Keating attends the Ridgefield game? Will she find out why I'm not playing? Will she think I'm an unreliable student and teammate? Will it hurt my chances of making the freshman team?

Layla's stomach dropped and tears stung her eyes. Her big plans and lifelong dreams seemed to be slipping away.

* * *

After the final bell, Layla checked the grading app. She was right. She had failed the test. She trudged to the locker room and stood in the doorway of Coach Eagan's office.

"Hi, Layla," Coach Eagan said from behind her desk.

"Hi, Coach."

"What's up? Why aren't you getting changed?"

"I can't," said Layla quietly.

"What do you mean?"

"I got a fifty-five on a big algebra test, and now my overall average is below a seventy percent."

Coach Eagan's face fell.

Before Coach could respond, Layla said, "But I have a plan. I'm meeting with Mrs. Fisher after school every day, starting today. When I'm ready, I'll retake the test. My average should go back up in time for the Washington game."

Coach Eagan nodded. "Well, obviously we'll miss you at the Ridgefield game tomorrow and next week's practices."

Layla could feel tears forming again. She swallowed hard.

"Do what you have to do and get back into the

game. The sooner the better," said Coach Eagan. "We could certainly use your serve against Washington."

"Will you tell the rest of the team?" asked Layla. "I have to meet Mrs. Fisher, and I don't want to be late. Plus, I don't think I can face them without losing it."

"I'll tell them," said Coach Eagan. "Chin up, Sanchez, okay?"

Layla nodded.

"Now, go learn why X left Y or whatever," said Coach.

Layla forced a slight smile but couldn't hold it when her teammates entered the locker room to change.

Filled with guilt and embarrassment, Layla lowered her head and weaved her way through them as she headed toward the door.

"Hey, Layla. Where are you going?" asked Kristy.

"I can't stay," she said.

"Wait . . . why?" asked Grace.

She shook her head and walked faster. "I'm so sorry," she said as she ran out.

CHAPTER 9

FINDING BALANCE

Layla walked slowly into Mrs. Fisher's classroom.

"Have a seat, Ms. Sanchez," said her teacher, "and please wipe that look off your face."

"What look?" asked Layla. She sat down on a nearby chair and hoisted her backpack on top of the desk.

"Like you'd rather walk on hot coals than be here with me."

"I'm sorry, Mrs. Fisher. It's nothing personal," said Layla.

"I understand," Mrs. Fisher said with a smile. "When I was your age, I hated going to physical education class as much as you hate algebra."

"Really?" asked Layla.

"Yes. I was never athletic, but I was a math whiz. You hate math, but you're an excellent athlete. We all have our strengths and weaknesses," said Mrs. Fisher. "I don't expect you to love math, but you have to get through it, just like I had to get through P.E. I still had to change and go out there and run around, even if I didn't want to."

Layla laughed at the thought of Mrs. Fisher as a middle school student huffing her way around the track.

"Tell me something—how'd you get through math before this year?" asked Mrs. Fisher.

"My dad used to help me," said Layla. "He died when I was in sixth grade. Teachers went easy on me that year, I think. They gave me less work and lots of extra time to finish assignments. Then last year in seventh grade, we had an extra teacher in the room. That helped."

"Does your mom help you?"

"She would if I asked her, but I haven't," said Layla. "Kristy offered to tutor me, but I used online help sites instead."

"And I didn't see you at the after-school sessions," Mrs. Fisher said.

Layla shook her head.

"So, you had help all around you, but you studied on your own. Why?"

"Coach Eagan talked to us about getting ready for high school, about learning how to balance school and sports," said Layla. "I thought I could do it, without my dad or anyone else helping me, but I couldn't."

"Did Coach Eagan say you had to learn this balancing trick by yourself?"

"No."

"Right, because she knows that nobody gets

anywhere without help from others," said Mrs. Fisher. "So, let me help you."

"Okay," said Layla.

"First, you need a new plan moving forward."

Layla nodded.

"What will you do differently from now on?" asked Mrs. Fisher.

"I'll ask more questions in class."

"Good," said Mrs. Fisher. "Go on."

"I'll see you during lunch or study hall if I need help."

Mrs. Fisher made a "continue" sign with her hand.

"I'll stay after school when you offer review sessions before the quizzes and tests," added Layla. "And I'll accept Kristy's offer to tutor me."

"Sounds like an excellent game plan," said Mrs. Fisher.

Layla smiled.

"Now, let's get to work."

Mrs. Fisher handed Layla a piece of paper with a word problem. It read: *Layla is a professional volleyball player. She has a contract that pays her a base rate of $1,275 per game. She earns an extra $225 for each ace she serves. At the last game, she earned $1,950. How many aces did she serve?*

"Seriously?" Layla said with a smile on her face.

"I bet you thought volleyball and algebra couldn't be friends."

Maybe they can be, Layla thought. *Maybe that's the key to this balancing trick—making connections.*

* * *

Layla attended the Ridgefield game with her mom to support her teammates. Nervous energy ran through her as she watched her teammates fight for every point.

When they started losing, she felt helpless and guilty. Her leg bounced out of control while she sat watching in the bleachers. She wanted to run onto the court.

Her mom placed a steadying hand on Layla's leg. "All you can do is keep cheering," said Mom.

Layla stood up and shouted, "Go, Lincoln!"

They played hard but lost their first game of the season.

Layla could hear Coach Eagan's supportive comments from the bleachers. "Great game, ladies. Chins up!"

"It's painful not being with them," said Layla.

"I know, but you'll work your way back onto the team," said her mom. "We all stumble, Layla. The important thing is that you get up and keep going."

The next week, Layla hustled each day from her last class to Mrs. Fisher's room instead of the gym. The change in routine felt strange at first, but she got used to it.

Kristy kept Layla updated with the team by telling her what happened at practice.

On Friday, Layla went to Mrs. Fisher's room during her study hall to retake the algebra test.

"How're you feeling, Ms. Sanchez?" asked Mrs. Fisher.

"Definitely more confident, but nervous too," said Layla.

"You have nothing to worry about," said Mrs. Fisher.

"How do you know?" Layla asked.

"I just know," she said as she handed the test to Layla.

Forty-five minutes later, Layla was done.

"Well?" asked Mrs. Fisher.

"Surprisingly, I feel good about this," said Layla.

"You shouldn't be surprised," said Mrs. Fisher. "You were prepared."

"Thanks for all of your help, Mrs. Fisher," Layla said.

"You're welcome, Ms. Sanchez," she said.

Layla headed toward the classroom door. Before

walking out, she turned around to ask Mrs. Fisher a question.

"I'm not a machine, Ms. Sanchez," Mrs. Fisher said, "but I know how important this is to you. I'll correct your test as soon as I can. Your grade should be posted by the end of the day."

Layla grinned. Mrs. Fisher had read her mind.

"Okay. Thanks," said Layla. She flashed a nervous smile before leaving.

Layla refreshed the grading app on her cell phone countless times throughout the school day. When the final bell rang, her grade still hadn't changed.

Layla took the bus home instead of going to the last practice before the big game against Washington Middle School.

When she checked an hour later, a message read: *The system will be updated from Friday at 4 p.m. to Saturday at 10 a.m.*

You've got to be kidding me! Layla thought.

She emailed both Mrs. Fisher and Coach Eagan

to see if they could help. All she could do now
was wait.

CHAPTER 10

GOOD NEWS

The next morning, the first thing Layla did was check her email.

Coach Eagan had responded: *Layla, I'll also check with Mrs. Fisher about your grade. Come to the game ready to play, just in case. We should know by the time you get there.*

Layla packed her sports bag and had breakfast with her mom before they drove to the school.

"I'm really proud of you, Layla," Mom said as she pulled into the crowded parking lot.

"For what? We don't even know if I did well enough on the test to play."

"But you worked hard this whole week. You gave it your best effort, which is all I ever ask," Mom said. "Your dad would've been proud of you too."

Layla let her comments soak in. A warmth spread through her. "Thanks, Mom."

As her mom looked for a parking space, Layla watched people walking toward the gym entrance. Because of the ongoing crosstown rivalry, fans went all out for this game. Some carried signs or painted their faces with their team's colors. Also, every year the principals came dressed up. Mr. Rivera, principal of Lincoln, dressed up as Abraham Lincoln in a dark suit, full black beard, and black top hat. Mrs. Mager from Washington dressed like George Washington in a white, ruffled shirt, black blazer, and white wig.

As Layla walked toward the gym, her mom said, "So, tell me, do you like math a little bit more now that you understand it better?"

"A little," Layla admitted.

"I knew it! My little mathematician!" her mom yelled.

"Don't get carried away, Mom," Layla said with a laugh. She saw players from Washington, already dressed in their blue and gold uniforms. As Layla looked around for her teammates, Kristy popped up by her side.

"Hey!" yelled Kristy. She gave Layla a quick hug. "Are you playing today?"

"I don't know yet," said Layla. "I'm still waiting on my algebra grade. I brought my gear just in case."

"We could really use you," said Kristy. She gave Layla another quick hug. "I have to get in there. Keep checking for your grade."

"I will," said Layla.

Kristy headed toward the locker room, while Layla and her mom headed toward the bleachers. The gym was filling up fast with excited fans on both sides. The two principals were taking pictures with students, and the school mascots playfully teased each other.

Layla's mom spotted a couple of empty seats on the Lions' side of the bleachers. "We should grab those before someone else does," she said.

"Hold on, Mom," Layla said. She took a deep breath and checked her email. She had one from Mrs. Fisher. The subject line was "Good news."

CHAPTER 11

BACK IN THE GAME

With trembling hands, Layla scanned the email.

I'm so sorry, Ms. Sanchez. I don't always check my school email once I leave for the weekend. I have a life too, you know! Anyway, you ACED the retake! 100! I averaged this with your first one (55). Your unit test grade is now a 78. See you at the game!

Layla jumped up and down and waved her arms at her mom. "I've got to go! I've got to go! I'm playing!"

Her mom did the same excited dance and yelled, "Yay! Go! Go!"

Layla turned and ran into the locker room. Kristy screamed as soon as she saw Layla.

"I passed! I'm playing!" Layla announced. She was crushed with hugs and bombarded with high-fives. She then quickly changed and joined her teammates' chant of "Lions! Lions! Lions!"

The crowd erupted when Layla and her teammates burst out of the locker room and onto the court. Players from both teams lined up and met at the net. The girls held one hand out, slapping the opposing players' hands as they walked down the line. The cheers were booming when the six starting players took their spots on each side of the court. Layla wasn't starting since she had missed a game and a week of practice.

"That's fair," she had told Coach Eagan. She meant it, but she was also itching to play.

The Hawks won the coin toss, so they served first.

The serve was low, just skimming the net. Kristy shuffled forward and bumped it back over the net.

The Hawks returned the ball with a traditional pass, set, spike play. Grace went down on one knee and held her arms out for the dig. She passed the ball with a solid bump to Talia near the net. Talia raised her arms and fingers and set the ball toward Ellie, who jumped up and attacked the ball with a mighty smack. A Hawks player fell on both knees and managed a solid return back over the net. Maggie jumped high and blocked the ball with her long, strong arms. The ball landed with a thud on the Hawks' side.

Lions' turn to serve!

The first set was intense, with each side diving and stretching for every point. The Lions led for a while, but then the Hawks came alive. When the score was tied at 22, and it was the Lions' turn to serve, Layla went into the game.

Layla moved into position. She breathed deeply in and out a few times to calm her nerves. She was excited to be back on the court. She was also nervous because Coach Keating was watching from the stands.

Most of all, she didn't want to let her team down again. She had already disappointed them by not being able to play against Ridgefield. This was her chance to make it up to them.

Layla scanned the other side of the court and decided where to aim it. She drowned out the noise from the crowd and focused on the ball in her hand. She bounced it a few times, twirled it in her hands, and took three steps back. The crowd cheered louder. They knew she was backing up for her jump serve. She could hear people yelling "Ace!" from the stands.

Layla tossed the ball high and in front of her. She jumped and hit the ball hard toward the Hawks' setter in the back row. The girl tried to get under it, but the ball bounced off her wrists and out of bounds.

Point for the Lions! 23–22.

Layla smiled wide. She was back! And it felt so good! Layla backed up and served again, this time to the outside hitter. The Hawks player made contact, but the ball flew right into the net.

Another point for the Lions. 24–22.

Layla served another strong ace to give the Lions the first set, 25–22. The gym exploded in cheers. As the teams switched sides on the court, Layla glanced over to the bleachers. Her mom waved at her. Mrs. Fisher gave her two thumbs up, and Coach Keating was taking notes. Layla flashed a big smile and then refocused.

Layla clapped her hands and shouted to her teammates, "Let's go, Lions!" As Layla looked at each of her teammates, she knew they were going to win. They stood in strong, ready positions and had determined looks on their faces. They were communicating, and their skills were sharper than they were at the start of the season. They were truly prepared.

The crowd's volume never decreased. The Hawks came back strong, winning the second set 27–25, but the Lions took the third, 15–10. The Lions won the match. Layla had savored every moment of the game.

After the game, Kristy and Layla walked side-by-side toward the locker room. Layla put her arm around Kristy's shoulder. "So, I was thinking about my plan to better balance sports and academics," Layla said.

"Yeah?" Kristy asked.

"I was thinking maybe you could tutor me in algebra, and I can help you with your serve," said Layla.

"Seriously?" Kristy said with a laugh. "That sounds so familiar. Whoever first thought of that plan is a genius!"

"Thank you," said Layla.

"You will not take credit for my brilliant idea, Layla Sanchez."

"Okay, fine, it was your idea," said Layla. "I admit it. I'll also admit that I really need the help. And let's face it, you really need help on your serve."

Layla and Kristy laughed as they headed into the locker room. The rest of the team was already there.

The girls bunched up together in between the lockers and jumped up and down at the same time.

They chanted, "Ace! Ace! Ace!" when Layla joined them. She smiled so hard her face hurt, but this win was a team effort. When she switched the chant to "Lions! Lions! Lions!" the other girls followed her lead.

ABOUT the AUTHOR

Cindy L. Rodriguez is the author of the YA novel *When Reason Breaks* and contributed to the anthology *Life Inside My Mind: 31 Authors Share Their Personal Struggles*. Before becoming a teacher, she was an award-winning reporter for *The Hartford Courant* and researcher for *The Boston Globe*'s Spotlight Team. She is a founder of and blogger at Latinxs in Kid Lit, which celebrates children's literature by/for/about Latinxs. Cindy is a big fan of the three Cs: coffee, chocolate, and coconut. She is currently a middle school reading specialist in Connecticut, where she lives with her family.

GLOSSARY

algebra (AL-juh-bruh)—a type of mathematics in which letters and symbols are used to represent numbers

confident (KON-fi-duhnt)—sure of oneself

execute (EK-suh-kyoot)—to perform or carry out

hustle (HUHS-uhl)—to work quickly and energetically

mascot (MAS-kot)—a person or animal that represents a sports team

mathematician (math-uh-muh-TISH-uhn)—a person who studies math

routine (roo-TEEN)—a regular way or pattern of doing tasks

savor (SAY-vur)—to enjoy or appreciate

session (SESH-uhn)—a period of time devoted to a certain activity

strategic (struh-TEE-jik)—relating to or showing the use of a plan to achieve a goal

topspin (TAHP-spin)—a forward spinning motion of a ball

DISCUSSION QUESTIONS

1. Layla excels in volleyball but struggles in her algebra class. Have you ever had trouble balancing academics and extra activities? What made it difficult? What did you do to balance everything?

2. We often avoid the things we do not enjoy, but this leads to consequences. Discuss the specific ways Layla avoids her algebra work and the consequences. Have you ever experienced something similar? What did you do? What should Layla have done differently?

3. Layla's problems with math are personal, but her actions affect others, including her coach and her teammates. Have you ever been a member of a team? Discuss the importance of thinking about your teammates even when dealing with individual problems.

WRITING PROMPTS

1. Layla is looking forward to moving on to high school, but she will miss her coach and teammates at Lincoln Middle School. Write a letter from Layla to next year's new middle school volleyball players. What advice would she give the sixth graders?

2. During the story, Layla helps sixth grader Grace with her volleyball skills. Write a few paragraphs from Grace's point of view. Pretend Grace is writing in her journal about her first season, and specifically, her interactions with Layla "Ace" Sanchez.

3. Both Mrs. Fisher and Layla's mom talk about how we all have strengths and weaknesses. Both, however, advocate for working through a problem. Write about a time that you didn't like something, or found it to be difficult, but later you ended up liking it.

LEARN THE TERMS

ace: a serve that cannot be returned by the other team

bump: to pass the volleyball with the forearms

dig: passing, usually by bumping, a fast-moving ball that is close to touching the court

dynamic stretches: active movements where joints and muscles go through a full range of motion

float serve: an overhand serve that causes the ball to change direction as it floats, like a knuckleball in baseball

jump serve: an overhand serve that creates topspin. The player makes contact with the ball by jumping to hit it.

libero: a defensive player who is responsible for receiving the attack or serve. The libero is usually the player with the quickest reaction time and best passing skills. Other volleyball positions are: setter, middle blocker/hitter, outside hitter/left-side hitter, opposite hitter/right-side hitter.

pass, set, spike: the first contact after a serve is considered a pass. The second contact is considered a set. It is usually a pass with the fingertips to set up a spike. Usually the third contact is a hit, attack, or spike. The player uses an open hand and swings at the ball to send it over the net.

platform: the player's forearms when they are put together by holding both hands together to create one larger surface for the ball

ready position: the flexed but comfortable posture a player assumes before moving to contact the ball

serve: one of the game's six basic skills; used to put the ball into play. It is the only skill controlled entirely by one player.

shuffle: to move one's feet along without lifting them fully from the ground